All the baby animals in the bush wish to cordially invite

....

to their fantastic beauty pageant!

Published in 2015 by Struik Lifestyle
(an imprint of Random House Struik (Pty) Ltd)
Company Reg. No 1966/003153/07
Estuaries No. 4, Century Avenue (Oxbow Crescent),
Century City, Cape Town
PO Box 1144, Cape Town 8000, South Africa

www.randomstruik.co.za

ISBN: 978-1-43230-429-4

Publisher: Linda de Villiers
Editor: Cecilia Barfield
Design manager: Beverley Dodd
Designer: Randall Watson
Illustrator: Jane Heinrichs

Reproduction: Hirt & Carter Cape (Pty) Ltd
Printing and binding: Tien Wah Press (Pte) Ltd, Malaysia

Lynn Bedford Hall is a well-known and experienced food
writer, award-winning author and journalist. This former
teacher has also written a few children's books. Her books
include, *inter alia*, *Hamlet and Pretoria*, *Fig Jam and Foxtrot*,
Best of Cooking in South Africa and *Fabulous Food*.

Jane Heinrichs is an award-winning children's book illustrator
with a BA in Art History and Classics from the University
of Manitoba (Distinction), an MA in Art History from
The Courtauld Institute of Art (Distinction) and an
MA in Illustration from Camberwell College of Art.

MATTIE'S MAGICAL ANIMAL DREAMWORLD #2

The Castle of Cupcakes

For my granddaughters
Anna, Alice and Charlotte
– LYNN BEDFORD HALL

For Mary, my baby daughter, whose
heartbeat inspired each brushstroke
– JANE HEINRICHS

Mattie lives on a farm deep in the heart of the country. It is a quiet place, far from any city. She has no brothers or sisters or friends, and so Mattie was very, very lonely. Until the night of **the secret**. A secret so precious, that only she and her magic, dreamworld animals know about it – and this is how it all began.

One day, Mattie and her mum were walking in the veld, when they saw a big, black beetle crawling under a stone. "Out with you!" her mum scolded. "You beetles eat my roses!" And she poked at it with a stick.

"Mum, no! You'll hurt it! Poor beetle." Bending down, Mattie pushed the stone aside, the beetle scurried away, and **that was the beginning**.

All day the beetle raced across the veld, telling every creature he met that Mattie had saved his life. "Her mother nearly crushed me with her stick! So let us all say thank you by inviting her into our animal world every night when she goes to sleep. We'll share make-believe adventures with her, put lovely dreams into her mind, and when she wakes she'll think of her new friends and never feel lonely again."

And guess what?

This was **the start** of Mattie's magical animal dreamworld adventures ...

Mattie was just nodding off to sleep
when she heard a knock at her window.
"Mattie! Mattie! It's your friend Goofy the Giraffe,
and I have some exciting news!"
"What is it, Goofy?" asked Mattie as she slipped out of bed.
"The animals are having a competition to see
who has the smartest, prettiest baby, and there will
be a grand prize for the winner. Come and see!
Just climb onto my back, hold on tight,
and we'll gallop to the farmyard."

Off they went, and there, in the pale after-noon light Mattie saw all the baby animals gathered in circles around their mothers, who were busily cleaning, polishing, brushing, buffing and combing their small families. Every mother wanted her children to win the grand prize, presented by the judge, Wiseman Owl.

"And what will that prize be?" Mattie asked.

Goofy smiled. "A **huge** surprise, Mattie! Just look!"

And there! Balanced on top of the old
farmyard table, towered an enormous,
brilliant Castle of Cupcakes, decorated in every colour
of the rainbow, and glittering with sprinkles.
"I was wondering about the prize," explained Wiseman,
"when I saw Betty Bear's bakery van pass. It was her last
Castle and she offered to sell it at a good price.
So I scooped it up, and here we are!"

Mattie slid off Goofy's back
and skipped around the circle of animals.
Polly Pig was rolling up, very tightly,
the tails of her eight little piglets, fastening them firmly
with clothes pegs. "Oooh Mum!" they squealed.
"Never mind, when those pegs come off you'll have the most
beautiful bunches of curls bobbing behind. Now wipe your
snouts and mind the mud, and you're sure to win.

"Oh no they won't!"
muttered Molly Meerkat.
"Just look at my babies, standing
straight in a row like soldiers, hanging their
hands down over their tummies,
their tails on the ground so that they don't fall over.
And they've promised not to eat any lizards today."
"And the sunglasses?" asked Polly.
"To keep the moonshine out of their eyes.
They don't like bright lights."

Then Mattie heard a loud snorting and rattling of quills. Patsy Porcupine's babies were not happy with what their mother was doing: she was plaiting the flurry of black and white hairs that porcupines have on their heads. "Sshh, my porkies. These little plaits will stand up all over, like lollipops, and you'll look good enough to eat!"

But then, oh dear! A small zebra ran past,
splattering them all with mud. "Oh I'm so sorry, Patsy,"
Zelda Zebra said, wringing her hooves.

"He might look like a donkey in pyjamas, but I think he's beautiful, and I was just polishing his stripes, when he bounced off to chat to the springbok lambs who were having their hides brushed and their horns rubbed up."

Just then, one jumpy little springbok
wanted to play. He took a giant leap,
and landed on top of a small mountain tortoise.
"Hey you!" shouted the tortoise's mum.
"I've just buffed my baby's creamy yellow shell to
look like sunshine!" and she flapped her duster across
the little buck's white face. "Now jump away
quickly so that I can get my baby ready."
This time Mattie wasn't listening.
Something was making her very frightened...

"Goofy, I can hear something angry and fierce behind that bush – and – and **here it comes**!" she cried.

Bellowing loudly, a ferocious buffalo burst into the farmyard. With his huge mouth and long, curved horns, he looked evil and greedy and, snorting loudly, he stamped right up to the table. With one big chomp the Castle was gone, icing flew everywhere, and all the babies were crying.

"Oh Goofy, this is terrible! What can we do?"
"I know **just** what we'll do," answered Goofy proudly.
Climb up onto my neck, Mattie, reach up high,
and together we'll gather a bagful of stars.
Look! The sky is alight with stars waiting
to be picked."

And in no time Mattie had plucked a bagful
of brilliant, shiny stars. "For the Mums."
"And the cupcakes, Mattie?"
"Wait and see..."

"Morning, love. Any dreams?"
asked Mattie's Mum next morning.
"Yes, Mum, I dreamt I was baking cupcakes."
"What fun, Mattie! I'll help you; but what are they for?"
"That's a **big secret**, Mum."
Together they baked all day,
building a glorious castle of cupcakes,
with silver balls and pink daisies all over.

When Mattie and Goofy
arrived in the farmyard that evening,
the animals were still upset; some of
the babies still sobbing…
"Surprise! Surprise!" called Mattie.
"Everyone has come first and won a prize!"

Wiseman handed out the stars and cupcakes,
and they all jumped with joy – except for the
wicked buffalo, but Mattie, being so kind,
found him behind a bush and handed him
a cupcake too. And then the party started!
"Oh Goofy! Look at them bouncing and dancing.
Let's join in the fun!"

And so they did, until the sun rose, and it was time for bed.

For another of Mattie's magical animal dreamworld adventures, read *Up, Up and AWAY!*.